Vole and Troll

Iza Trapani

Charlesbridge

For JUNE and EVA
with all my love

Troll's song may be sung to the
tune of "This Old Man."

At the time of publication, all URLs printed in this book were accurate and active.
Charlesbridge and the author are not responsible for the content or accessibility of any website.

Library of Congress Cataloging-in-Publication Data
Names: Trapani, Iza, author, illustrator.
Title: Vole and troll / Iza Trapani.
Description: Watertown, MA : Charlesbridge, [2019] | Summary: A clever vole distracts a grumpy,
hungry, and musical troll who threatens to eat him by teaching the troll new songs, and in the end
they become good friends because two voices are better than one.
Identifiers: LCCN 2018033258 (print) | LCCN 2018034788 (ebook) | ISBN 9781632897480 (ebook) |
ISBN 9781632897497 (ebook pdf) | ISBN 9781580898850 (reinforced for library use)
Subjects: LCSH: Voles—Juvenile fiction. | Trolls—Juvenile fiction. |
Singing—Juvenile fiction. | Friendship—Juvenile fiction. | CYAC:
Voles—Fiction. | Trolls—Fiction. | Singing—Fiction. |
Friendship—Fiction. | LCGFT: Picture books.
Classification: LCC PZ7.T6867 (ebook) | LCC PZ7.T6867 Vo 2019 (print) | DDC
[E]—dc23
LC record available at https://lccn.loc.gov/2018033258

Published by Charlesbridge
85 Main Street
Watertown, MA 02472
(617) 926-0329
www.charlesbridge.com

Printed in China
(hc) 10 9 8 7 6 5 4 3 2 1

Illustrations done in watercolor, colored pencil, and ink
Display type and text font set in Franklin Gothic Hand Light by Gert Wiescher
Color separations by Colourscan Print Co Pte Ltd, Singapore
Printed by 1010 Printing International Limited in Huizhou, Guangdong, China
Production supervision by Brian G. Walker
Designed by Joyce White

Vole headed to a knoll across the creek to sample the tastiest grass in the valley. But a gruff and greedy troll was said to guard the bridge.

Sure enough, Troll was at the bridge, singing.

Troll-dee-roll, I'm a troll,
And my favorite food is vole.
With a knick-knack, paddywhack,
Better pay the toll,
Or you'll end up in my bowl!

"Oh, my!" Vole said. "Your voice is so clear and deep.
Please sing me another song."

"Huh?" said Troll. "This is the only song I know."

"Then I'll teach you a new one," said Vole.

"OK, but you'll still owe me a toll," said Troll.

Vole taught Troll "The Itsy Bitsy Spider."

The itsy bitsy spider
Climbed up the waterspout.
Down came the rain
And washed the spider out.

Out came the sun
And dried up all the rain,
And the itsy bitsy spider
Climbed up the spout again.

Troll sang and moved his fingers to and fro, to and fro.
He concentrated so hard that he didn't see Vole sneak off
to the knoll.

THAT VOLE!

THAT VOLE!

HE'S OUT OF CONTROL!

I'LL PUT HIM IN MY BOWL!

A few days later, Vole returned for more of that tasty grass. Again Troll popped out singing.

Troll-dee-roll, I'm a troll,

And my favorite food is vole.

With a knick-knack, paddywhack,

Better pay the toll,

Or you'll end up in my bowl!

"You!" Troll yelled. "Pay me or I'll gobble you up!"

"I can't pay," Vole told Troll, "but I can teach you another song."

"Oh, no! You won't fool me again!" Troll bellowed.
Vole said, "Don't worry. In this song you won't have
to use your fingers or hands."

Troll, being a musical soul, could not resist.
Vole taught him "The Hokey-Pokey."

You put your right foot in.

You take your right foot out.
You put your right foot in,
And you shake it all about.

You do the hokey-pokey,
And you turn yourself around.
That's what it's all about.

And just as Troll turned himself around,
Vole scuttled off to the knoll for a feast of
grassy greens.

In a few days Vole came back, and as usual,
Troll was singing.

Troll-dee-roll, I'm a troll,

And my favorite food is vole.

With a knick-knack, paddywhack,

Better pay the toll,

Or you'll end up in my bowl!

"You tricked me twice and that's not nice!" Troll blared. "I will gobble you up right now!"

"Oh, please don't be mad. You're such a great singer. Let me teach you another song," Vole said.

Troll snapped, "No, you don't! Not again!"

"Don't worry," Vole told him. "You won't have to use your fingers, hands, *or* legs."

Troll was too curious not to try. Vole began to sing.

*If you're happy
and you know it,
clap your hands—*

"No! No! No!" Troll boomed. "You said no hands.
Besides, I'm NOT happy!"
So Vole changed the words.

If you're grumpy and you know it, nod your head.

If you're grumpy and you know it, nod your head.

If you're grumpy and you know it,

And you really want to show it,

If you're grumpy and you know it, nod your head.

Troll sang, nodding his head up and down so much
that he made himself dizzy.

Once more, Vole was able to scurry away.

THAT VOLE! THAT VOLE!

HE'S OUT OF CONTROL!

I'LL PUT HIM IN MY BOWL!

I'LL EAT HIM ON A ROLL!

I'LL MAKE FILLET OF VOLE!

I'LL HAVE A HEAPING HELPING
OF A CASSEROLE OF VOLE!

The next time Vole arrived, Troll snatched him by the tail.

Vole begged, "Please wait! Before you gobble me up, would you sing your Troll-dee-roll song one more time?"

"Huh?" said Troll, confused. Was Vole trying to trick him again?

It was true—Vole *had* tricked his way to the knoll several times. That grass was simply too delicious to resist. But Vole also loved teaching Troll new songs and hearing Troll's deep, delightful voice.

"Please," said Vole. "It would be my last happiness to hear you sing."

So Troll sang his song, and Vole joined in with a sweet, high harmony.

Troll-dee-roll, I'm a troll,
And my favorite food is vole.
With a knick-knack, paddywhack,
Better pay the toll,
Or you'll end up in my bowl!

They filled the valley with music so enchanting that fish sprang
from the creek, flapping their fins with pleasure. Moles rolled out
of their holes to celebrate. Even the songbirds hushed to listen.

Troll, too, was overjoyed. Never had he heard such beautiful sounds. No one had ever sung with him before. He threw his hands to his once-lonely heart and sighed.

Vole began to run, but he stopped when he saw Troll's beaming face.

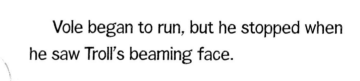

"What kind of singing was that?" Troll asked in wonder.
"That was a duet. Two voices singing different parts
and making a whole new sound," Vole said.
"Again!" Troll cried out. "Let's sing it again!"

Vole smiled at Troll and said, "I will gladly sing with you, but please, let's make up some new words."
And they did.

Troll-dee-roll, by the knoll,

We're a lucky vole and troll.

With a knick-knack, paddywhack,

Happy as can be,

Singing perfect harmony!